Love Dragon

Joan Morrison

Illustrations by

Stanley Morrison

Illustrations copyright 2017 by Stanley Morrison
stanleymorrisonart.com

ISBN: 1546318984
ISBN-13: 978-1546318989
Library of Congress Control Number: 2017916008
CreateSpace Independent Publishing Platform, North Charleston, SC

Contents

LOVE DRAGON

1
LOVE DRAGON

Love Dragon helped Grandma make a batch of dragon juice. "Tell me again how much Mommy and Daddy love me," Love Dragon said.

Grandma opened her wings as far as they would go and said, "They love you this much. In fact, you're loved so much it's known throughout the land."

Grandma laughed and hugged little Love Dragon. She said, "That's why you're so happy."

Just then Papa raced into the cave.

He said, "We've been summoned by Royal Dragon to help stop a raging forest fire. It's the worst fire we've ever had, and it's spreading fast. We'll be back in a couple of days."

He raced out of the cave and was gone.

Love Dragon crunched up his face and asked, "How can Mama and Papa put out a fire? We're fire-breathing dragons and cause fires when we sneeze."

Grandma put her wing around the little dragon.

She said, "When fires are out of control, we can use our wide wings to help direct the flames."

"I want Mama," said Love Dragon, and he began to sniffle.

"I want Papa!" Love Dragon screeched and squeaked.

Grandma scooped Love Dragon up.

"What's wrong, sweetie?" she asked.

Love Dragon sniffled. "Mama and Papa don't really love me. If they did, they wouldn't have left me."

Grandma hugged him close. "Oh, Love Dragon, your parents love you very much, and so do Grandpa and I."

Grandpa heard the ruckus from outside and came into the cave.

He said, "Grandson, sometimes we're called away and have to leave our loved ones behind. It doesn't mean that we don't love them. It means there's something very important that needs to be done, and we're honored to help."

Love Dragon didn't care about honor. But he was too tired to keep screeching. Every now and then, he whimpered as Grandma gently rocked him to sleep.

The next morning Love Dragon felt empty inside. Grandma was busy around the cave, and Grandpa was diving for fish in the lake.

Hmm, Love Dragon wondered. If Grandma is right and my parents do love me, they wouldn't leave me so sad.

Love Dragon thought and thought, and then his eyes opened wide.

"That's it!" he said. "They were in such a hurry that they forgot to leave me any love. I've got to find my parents. I'll get some love from them and bring it back."

The little dragon wished he could fly. It would be so much quicker to find his parents, but his wings were still too small. He tried to fly every day. Each time he would smash into trees and rocks, landing hard. His parents told him to be patient.

So off he walked in search of his parents.

2
INTO THE FOREST

At the entrance to the forest, he was met by a watermelon dragon guarding the forest path.

"Halt," said the watermelon dragon. "You must read the rules of the forest."

Chiseled in a large tree were the forest rules. Fire-breathing dragons and forests didn't go very well, so Royal Dragon had made up rules to help protect the forest.

WATERMELON DRAGON

Love Dragon read each rule very carefully and pointed to each rule with his wing as he read. "Rule one, watermelon dragons protect the forest from fire. Rule two, fire-breathing dragons must have a watermelon dragon escort. Rule three, when a fire-breathing dragon sneezes, all dragons must yell 'Help! Fire!'"

The watermelon dragon pointed to the second rule on the list and said, "Fire-breathing dragons must not enter the forest without a watermelon dragon escort. You are a fire-breathing dragon, are you not?"

Love Dragon replied, "Yes, but I am too young to breathe fire."

The watermelon dragon looked him up and down and then said, "Hmm, give me one big cough, and I may let you enter."

Love Dragon coughed as hard as he could. Not even a tiny puff of smoke came out. He posed no danger entering the forest alone.

"You may enter, young dragon. Stay safe from the fires," the watermelon dragon said and waved him through.

FOREST RULES

3
STRAWBERRY DRAGON

Grumble. Rumble. Love Dragon hadn't gone far when his stomach told him he was hungry. He knew the forest was rich with food and water, so he raised his snout and sniffed.

"Ah, something sweet," Love Dragon said, and he followed the scent. He came to the area of the forest where the berries grow. Then he saw the most colorful berry dragons. He had heard stories of these berry dragons, but he'd never seen one before.

"Greetings!" said the berry dragons. There was a strawberry dragon, a raspberry dragon, a blueberry dragon, and a blackberry dragon.

"Hi! I'm Love Dragon. I'm very hungry. May I have some of your berries?"

"Yes," they all yelled.

The berry dragons pushed one another out of the way.

"Take mine! I have the best berries of all," each yelled.

They all pushed and shoved one another, and berries went flying everywhere.

STRAWBERRY DRAGON

Love Dragon tasted berries from them all.

"Yum!" he said. "They're all delicious."

All the berry dragons were chattering about their berries when the strawberry dragon got very quiet. He stared at Love Dragon and tilted his head side to side.

Then the strawberry dragon said, "We've heard of you, Love Dragon. Will you share your love with us?"

"I'm sorry," said Love Dragon as tears welled up in his eyes. "I don't have any right now. I'm off to the fires to get some."

"You get love from fire?" exclaimed the berry dragons all at once.

"No," said Love Dragon. He explained how his parents were fighting the fire and had accidently taken his love and how he was going to get it. The berry dragons looked at one another and nodded that they understood.

Love Dragon thanked them for the berries and started down the path.

The berry dragons waved and shouted, "Bring us back some love!"

4
THE OVAL ROCK

Love Dragon was very sad as he walked along the path. He had never been without love before, and he didn't like it.

Mama and Papa are going to be so happy to see me, thought Love Dragon.

He wasn't paying attention and kicked something in his way. It went rolling up the path. Love Dragon ran up to inspect it.

It was very pretty and looked like an oval rock. It shimmered in the sunlight.

What could this possibly be? thought Love Dragon.

He picked it up and noticed that it was very light. It felt hollow inside and was almost spongy on the outside.

He kicked it again, just to see how far it would roll, and it rolled down into a ravine. He peered over the ravine and wished he hadn't kicked it. He let out a really big sigh and went on his way.

THE OVAL ROCK

~ 12 ~

Anxious to reach the fires, Love Dragon hurried along the path.

Whap!

Something hit him on the back of his head.

"Ouch!" yelled Love Dragon.

Whap!

Something hit him on the back of his head again and knocked him over. He thought he saw something rolling and heard laughter fading in the distance.

Whackalala birds were flying above.

"Those rascals are dive-bombing me!" He shouted, "Stop that, you whackalala birds!"

The birds flew away.

WHACKALALA BIRD

5

DRAGON BEAST

Rubbing his head, Love Dragon marched on. As he came upon a curve in the path, he heard branches breaking behind him. A dragon beast jumped out of the brush. The dragon beast screeched, and Love Dragon screeched.

Love Dragon ran as fast and as far as his little legs could take him. When he couldn't run anymore, he rolled into a ball and hid under his little wings. He was so scared that he was shaking.

He remembered his papa telling him about dragon beasts.

"They are the largest dragons in the land, but they are gentle dragons," his papa had said.

Love Dragon peeked out from under his wings and was happy not to see a dragon beast.

He thought, Dragon beasts are not gentle at all.

DRAGON BEAST

~ 16 ~

6
ODD DRAGON

As Love Dragon caught his breath, he heard the sweetest sound. He decided to follow it. It got louder and louder as he walked, until before him stood the oddest dragon.

"What are you?" asked the odd dragon.

"I am Love Dragon."

"Oh," said the odd dragon. "I've heard of you, Love Dragon. Can you show me your love?"

Love Dragon looked at the ground and pouted. He told the odd dragon the whole story.

The odd dragon gasped.

"That is terrible," the odd dragon said. "I am a music dragon, my name is Banjobo, and if I could not share my music, I would be lost!"

"I know just how to cheer you up. I can give you my music," said Banjobo. He started strumming his strings, and Love Dragon liked it.

Then some more odd dragons came out from behind the trees. Each one could make music that sounded a little different.

BANJOBO

The music dragons would each shout, "Listen to my music, Love Dragon," and then play louder. Each kept playing louder and harder until Love Dragon could not take it anymore.

Love Dragon yelled, "Stop!"

But they didn't hear him. Love Dragon covered his ears with his wings and ran down the path. It was a horrible noise.

7
STINKY DRAGON

No sooner did Love Dragon get away from the noise than his nose began to twitch. A strong, stinky scent filled the air. He buried his snout under his wing. The smell got stronger and stronger.

A dragon stepped out from behind a bush and said, "Hi, I'm Violet."

Love Dragon backed away. "Stop! Don't come any closer!" Love Dragon said. The little dragon's eyes began to water and sting.

Love Dragon asked, "Why are you so stinky?"

Violet tilted her head and replied, "I am an onion dragon. Everyone knows that I am a strong and tangy delight. If you don't like it, then you do not have the acquired taste."

"Well, I don't like it. Stay away from me," said Love Dragon. He walked around her and then raced up the path.

Violet ran after the little dragon.
"But I just want to be friends!" she yelled.

Love Dragon ran faster and faster until the smelly dragon was far enough away.

ONION DRAGON
VIOLET

~ 21 ~

8
THREE-HEADED DRAGON

When Love Dragon stopped running from the onion dragon, he realized he had finally made it all the way to the fire.

He was so happy to see that the fires were out. All kinds of dragons were resting from their hard work.

Love Dragon looked everywhere for his parents, but he did not see them. "I am Love Dragon, and I'm looking for my parents," he said to a group of dragons.

"I know your parents," said the three-headed pepper dragon. "They are helping the watermelon dragons find the remaining hot spots."

Love Dragon was so disappointed that his parents weren't there. At the same moment, one of the heads of the three-headed pepper dragon started to sneeze.

"Aaaaaaaah aaaaaaaah"

"No!" yelled all the other dragons. "Don't sneeze! You'll cause a fire."

"No worries," said one of the other heads of the pepper dragon. "We don't sneeze fire." All the dragons let out a big sigh of relief.

THREE-HEADED PEPPER DRAGON

Then the pepper dragon sneezed. "Ahhhhhh *chooood!*"

Pepper dragons did not sneeze fire; they sneezed pepper, and pepper went everywhere. This caused all the fire dragons to sneeze fire.

All the dragons were running around sneezing. Some were sneezing fire, and all were yelling, "Help! Fire!"

Love Dragon was so scared that he would burn up that he ran away as fast as he could.

9
SPARKLY DRAGON

Love Dragon had never felt so loveless. Tired from walking and running and so disappointed that he had not found his parents, he began to cry.

"There, there, Love Dragon. Everything will be OK," said the sweetest voice the little dragon had ever heard.

Love Dragon spun around and thought, A fairy? They're not real. The little dragon closed his eyes tightly and then opened them.

"You are a fairy!" Love Dragon said. "Yes, I am," said the fairy. "I'm Gwendolyn. Why are you crying?"

Love Dragon wiped his tears and said, "I have no love. I went to the fires to find my parents. They left without leaving me love, so I went to go get some. But they weren't there."

Gwendolyn's eyes twinkled. She said, "You don't need to find anyone to have love. You only need to give love to have love."

Love Dragon burrowed his brows and scratched his head.

"But I don't have any love to give," he said. "That's why I'm going to get some."

GWENDOLYN

Gwendolyn smiled. "You don't need to find anyone to have love. You only need to give love to have love," she repeated.

Love Dragon rustled his wings and said, "This is too confusing! I'm the Love Dragon, and I don't have love to give. That is why I must go get it."

The fairy smiled. "If you want love, you only need to give love to have love."

Love Dragon tried so hard to understand.

He said, "You have to give love you don't have, to get love that you don't have, to have love that you don't need to get, because you gave it to have it?"

The fairy smiled and said again, "If you want love, you only need to give love to have love."

Love Dragon hit his head with his wing and said, "I'm too confused!"

The fairy said, "Whom would you like to give love to?"

"Me!" shouted Love Dragon. "I need love."

"OK," Gwendolyn said, chuckling. "Let me show you. Let's give your love to your mama and papa. You can give love to anyone or anything, and you can do it anywhere at any time. They don't need to be near you. Now close your eyes and imagine you're hugging your mama and papa."

Love Dragon wrapped his wings tightly around himself. When he opened his eyes, sparkles surrounded him. He had never felt so loved and happy.

"It's magic!" he whispered. He twirled around and around in the sparkles. He had never felt so good.

Suddenly the sparkles disappeared.

Love Dragon said, "Hey, how come I didn't see sparkles with my parents? That must mean they don't really love me."

Love Dragon started to sob. "Oh no," said Gwendolyn.

She put her hand on the little dragon's head and said, "We feel the love sparkles; we don't see them. I only let you see the sparkles so that you'd be able to see that love is all around you.

"You will see the sparkles only while you're with me. When you give love, the sparkles will appear. When you don't give love, they'll disappear."

A smile grew across Love Dragon's face. He gave love to the trees, to the butterflies, to the clouds, and to everything else near him. Sparkles swirled around him.

"Giving love is so much fun," said Love Dragon as he danced in the sparkles.

"Now," said Gwendolyn, "it's time for you to go back to your grandparents. They'll be worried about you. I'll take you there."

SPARKLY LOVE DRAGON

10
GARDEN DRAGONS

Gwendolyn and Love Dragon walked happily along the path as Love Dragon played in his love sparkles. After walking a while, the little dragon began to rub his eyes. He said, "Onion Dragon? Are you here?"

The stinky dragon came out from a bush. Love Dragon hid his snout under his wing.

"I told you to stay away from me," Love Dragon said. Love Dragon hadn't noticed that his sparkles had disappeared. Onion Dragon lowered her head.

"Hello, Violet. It's good to see you again," said Gwendolyn to the onion dragon. "Come with me."

She guided Violet down a small side path and said, "Love Dragon, you stay here."

The little dragon's eyes stopped burning, and a wonderful aroma came from the side path. It made him realize that he was very hungry.

Gwendolyn came back with Violet, but they brought friends. There was a broccoli dragon, a carrot dragon, a turnip dragon, and a peapod dragon. Love Dragon was very excited to meet so many new friends.

MIXED GARDEN DRAGONS

Violet handed Love Dragon a big bowl and said, "We made you a mixed garden salad."

The smell was wonderful. The little dragon ate everything in the bowl.

"Thank you! That was the most delicious meal I ever had," Love Dragon said. He knew that the onion made it tangy and special.

"I have the acquired taste." Love Dragon squealed with joy.

"I'm sorry I ran away before," said Love Dragon. "Now that your smell doesn't bother me, we can be friends. I hope to see you again."

Sparkles twirled around Love Dragon as he waved good-bye.

11
MUSIC DRAGONS

As Gwendolyn and Love Dragon came around the bend, they started to hear sounds from the music dragons. "Cover your ears, Gwendolyn," said Love Dragon. "It's going to get really noisy."

The music dragons all stated making music. Banjobo the banjo dragon strummed like crazy. There was Hermie the harmonica dragon playing way too fast, and Boomer the drum dragon played too fast and too loud.

"Oh dear," said Gwendolyn as she raised her hand to quiet the music dragons.

She pointed to each dragon one at a time and said to each, "Please play your melody quietly."

Each did and it was beautiful.

Then Gwendolyn said, "Now play at the same time but quietly so that all your melodies can be heard the same." They played the most beautiful sounds ever heard. Banjobo, Hermie, and Boomer had no idea they could sound so good together.

"Look!" shouted Love Dragon. "Everyone is sparkling."

Gwendolyn gently guided Love Dragon back to the path. It was time to go home.

"Thank you for bringing us back some love, Love Dragon," sang the music dragons.

MUSIC DRAGONS

~ 35 ~

12
MELON DRAGONS

As Gwendolyn and Love Dragon walked, something hit the little dragon in the back of his head and almost knocked him over. Whatever hit him went rolling and laughing into nearby bushes.

"Not again!" cried Love Dragon as his sparkles disappeared. "It's those pesky whackalala birds. They're dive-bombing me!"

Gwendolyn looked up and said, "There aren't any birds around. Are you sure it's them?"

"It's got to be," said Love Dragon. "They were flying above me last time this happened."

"You know," said Gwendolyn, "if you didn't see them hit you, it may not be them. You shouldn't accuse unless you're absolutely sure."

Gwendolyn walked off into the bushes and came out with a cantaloupe dragon and a honeydew dragon.

"Did you hit Love Dragon in the head?" she asked. The guilty looking melon dragons looked down.

"Yes," said the cantaloupe dragon. "It was an accident."

CANTALOUPE AND HONEYDEW DRAGONS

"We're trying to fly," said the honeydew dragon. "We get airborne but quickly fall. We curl into a ball for a softer landing. It makes landing fun. We're sorry we hit you."

Instead of getting angry, Love Dragon flapped his wings and replied, "Me, too. I've been trying to fly and keep falling and crashing into things. Would you show me how to curl up for a safe landing?"

The melon dragons showed Love Dragon to curl and roll.

"Thank you," said the little dragon. "I'm glad you fell into me!"

13
SPARKLY BEAST

Sparkles whirled around Love Dragon as he waved good-bye to the melon dragons. Love Dragon continued to fly, curl, and roll. He screeched with laughter. Then he smacked into something hard and rolled right into the ravine.

When Love Dragon unrolled himself, he knew he was in the ravine. He looked up and peering over the ravine edge was the dragon beast.

"Screech," said the dragon beast.

"Screech," squeaked Love Dragon.

Love Dragon was so scared that he grabbed the first thing he could find to hide himself with. It was the pretty, oval rock he had kicked down the ravine earlier. That seemed to make dragon beast screech louder.

Gwendolyn joined Love Dragon in the ravine and said to him, "Don't be scared. Dragon beasts are the gentlest dragons of all."

Love Dragon peeked out and snorted, "That dragon is not gentle."

The fairy took the pretty, oval rock from Love Dragon. "This is a dragon egg," she said as she floated up to the dragon beast.

As soon as dragon beast held it, he sparkled. There were more sparkles coming from the dragon beast than Love Dragon had ever seen.

"Dragon beasts are gentle, and that is why they are in charge of protecting dragon eggs," explained Gwendolyn.

Love Dragon finally understood that dragon beasts were truly gentle giants and that this dragon was only protecting the dragon egg.

SPARKLY DRAGON BEAST

14
MIXED BERRIES

Love Dragon and Gwendolyn continued down the path. Soon they smelled sweet berries.

"Let's stop so that I can get some berries to bring back to Grandma," said the little dragon.

Shoving one another out of the way, the berry dragons raced over to Love Dragon.

"Eat my berries. I have the best," they all yelled. The shoving quickly turned into berry throwing. Berries flew everywhere. Splat!

When they hit Gwendolyn, she raised her hand. The dragons stopped, and so did Love Dragon's sparkles.

The fairy brought a large bowl to each dragon. She asked that they all put some of their berries in it. When the bowl was full, she mixed the berries with a wave of her hand. She then gave a scoop of mixed berries to all the dragons, including Love Dragon.

"Yum!" said the berry dragons. "Our berries taste better mixed together."

MIXED BERRY DRAGONS

"Next time I'll bring my grandma. She'll show you how to make dragon juice," he said. Love Dragon put the rest of the mixed berries in a sack.

"Oh," Love Dragon continued. "I brought you lots of love! Can you feel it?"

All the berry dragons felt it. They all sparkled.

The little dragon and Gwendolyn said good-bye. Sparkles soared around Love Dragon.

15
SPARKLY GRANDMA

Soon Love Dragon saw his grandparents' cave.

As Love Dragon walked by the entrance of the forest, he noticed that a new forest rule was freshly scratched on the forest rules sign.

Pepper dragons must stay far away from fire-breathing dragons.

This made him very happy. It would help protect the forest from fires, and his parents wouldn't be called away.

NEW FOREST RULE

Grandma rushed out of the cave and hugged him tightly.

"We were so worried," she said. "You should never go off without telling us." Grandma and Love Dragon were surrounded with sparkles.

"Yes," said Grandpa. "I thought you had learned to fly and had flown away. Where were you?"

Love Dragon told the whole story of his adventure. He didn't stop once, not even to take a breath. As he finished his story, Love Dragon said, "Oh, I want you to meet Gwendolyn the fairy."

He turned around, but she wasn't there.

The little dragon's heart sank. He noticed that his sparkles faded away also. Then he remembered what Gwendolyn had taught him, and his heart felt full.

"The best thing about my adventure is I learned that to feel love, I simply have to give love," Love Dragon said and hugged both his grandparents as tightly as he could.

Love Dragon handed Grandma the sack of berries, and they went in to make dragon juice. Love Dragon happily helped Grandma.

Then he noticed sparkles dancing around Grandma. She was grabbing the sparkles and adding them to the dragon juice.

SPARKLY GRANDMA

How can that be? thought Love Dragon. The fairy said I wouldn't see love sparkles. "Grandma, do you see the sparkles?" shouted Love Dragon, all excited.

Grandma winked and said, "How do you think I put love into every batch?" Just then Love Dragon saw Gwendolyn come out from behind Grandma. "Even fairies can't resist dragon juice," said Gwendolyn as she waved good-bye.

Before Love Dragon could say anything more, Grandpa came in and whisked him away.

"Come on, little fella," Grandpa said. "Show me that curl and roll."

It didn't matter if Love Dragon could see love sparkles or not; he knew that if he gave love, they were there.

ABOUT THE AUTHOR

Joan Morrison lives in Florida, with her husband, Stan, and their two huskies. She enjoys nature, animals, the arts, hiking, holistic living, and spirituality. She has a degree in Computer Information Systems and is currently attending the Institute of Integrative Nutrition.

Her husband's dragons have so much character that they inspired her to write *Love Dragon*. This is her first book.

https://www.facebook.com/Love.Dragon.JMorrison

Made in the USA
San Bernardino, CA
19 July 2018